You Can't Have a Picnic at Night!

An Ivy and Mack story

T0327763

Written by Juliet Clare Bell
Illustrated by Gustavo Mazali
with Camilla Galindo

Collins

What's in this story?

Listen and say

moon

Download the audio at www.collins.co.uk/839668

stars

lights

 Ivy was happy. Today was picnic day in the forest with her friend Mina, Grandpa and Banjo the dog.

"Mack!" said Ivy. "Let's get dressed. It's the picnic with Mina and Grandpa this afternoon."

Ivy and Mack went shopping with Dad. They bought the food for their picnic. Ivy chose pineapple, watermelon and cheese. Mack chose chocolate and biscuits.

"This is yummy food for our picnic," said Mack.

"Oh dear! Where are the car keys?" said Dad. Ivy called Mum.

"Quick, Mum!" said Ivy. "Please bring *your* keys!"

They waited for Mum.

"I hate waiting," said Ivy. "Mina is waiting, too!"

"I'm waiting, too!" said Mack. "I'm hungry!"

Mum came on her bike with the keys.

"Let's go," said Ivy. "Mina is waiting for us and our picnic!"

Ivy and Mack washed the fruit and made the salad.

"Quick, Dad! Finish the sandwiches," said Ivy.

"Yes! I'm making them. But I need to do this work, too!" said Dad.

Mum was on the phone.

"I'm sorry, Ivy. But Mina can't come to the picnic."

"Oh no!" said Ivy. "Why not?"

"She fell and hurt her arm."

Ivy was sad. "Everything is going wrong!"

Mum was on the phone ... again.

"Hi Dad," said Mum. "What? Your washing machine? What's the problem? There's water on the kitchen floor? Oh no! I can fix it for you. See you in ten minutes!"

"Don't go, Mum," said Ivy. "It's our picnic day."

"I would like our picnic," said Mack.

"Sorry, Ivy. Sorry, Mack," said Mum. "Grandpa needs me."

"No Mina. No Mum. No sandwiches. No Grandpa. No Banjo the dog. This is a bad picnic day," said Ivy.

Ivy and Mack were sad.

"I know!" said Ivy. "Let's have the picnic this *evening*! In our garden!"

"You can't have a picnic at *night*!" said Mack.

"**We** can!" said Ivy.

"We can make the picnic. We don't need Mum and Dad to help," said Ivy.

"Yes! We can do it," said Mack.

Ivy went to her bedroom. She came down with a big bag.

"Mack! Come with me," she said.

Ivy and Mack put a rug on the ground.
They put lots of small lights on the tree.
They carried the picnic things from the
kitchen and put them on the rug.

Mum came home and Dad finished his work. Ivy and Mack showed them the garden.

"It's fantastic!" said Dad. "Well done, Ivy! Well done Mack!"

"What a beautiful picnic," said Mum. "There's only one more thing we need."

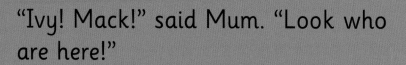

"Ivy! Mack!" said Mum. "Look who
are here!"

"Mina!" said Ivy.

"Grandpa and Banjo," said Mack.

Mack clapped his hands. "Look! There are stars in the trees, too!"

"Look!" said Ivy. "It's the moon!"

"You *CAN* have a picnic at night!" said Mack. "And he went to sleep."

Picture dictionary

Listen and repeat

picnic

pineapple

rug

salad

sandwich

watermelon

1 Look and order the story

2 Listen and say

Collins

Published by Collins
An imprint of HarperCollins*Publishers*
Westerhill Road
Bishopbriggs
Glasgow
G64 2QT

HarperCollins*Publishers*
1st Floor, Watermarque Building
Ringsend Road
Dublin 4
Ireland

William Collins' dream of knowledge for all began with the publication of his first book in 1819.

A self-educated mill worker, he not only enriched millions of lives, but also founded a flourishing publishing house. Today, staying true to this spirit, Collins books are packed with inspiration, innovation and practical expertise. They place you at the centre of a world of possibility and give you exactly what you need to explore it.

© HarperCollins*Publishers* Limited 2020

10 9 8 7 6 5 4 3 2

ISBN 978-0-00-839668-8

Collins® and COBUILD® are registered trademarks of HarperCollins*Publishers* Limited

www.collins.co.uk/elt

British Library Cataloguing in Publication Data

A catalogue record for this publication is available from the British Library.

Author: Juliet Clare Bell
Lead illustrator: Gustavo Mazali (Beehive)
Copy illustrator: Camilla Galindo (Beehive)
Series editor: Rebecca Adlard
Publishing manager: Lisa Todd
Product managers: Jennifer Hall and Caroline Green
In-house editor: Alma Puts Keren
Project manager: Emily Hooton
Editor: Deborah Friedland
Proofreaders: Natalie Murray and Michael Lamb
Cover designer: Kevin Robbins
Typesetter: 2Hoots Publishing Services Ltd
Audio produced by id audio, London
Reading guide author: Julie Penn
Production controller: Rachel Weaver
Printed and bound by: GPS Group, Slovenia

MIX
Paper from
responsible sources

FSC www.fsc.org **FSC** C007454

This book is produced from independently certified FSC™ paper to ensure responsible forest management.

For more information visit: **www.harpercollins.co.uk/green**

Download the audio for this book and a reading guide for parents and teachers at www.collins.co.uk/839668